This book belongs to

_____

_____

First published in 2011 in German under the title *Aschenputtel*
This English edition published by Floris Books in 2013
© 2011 NordSüd Verlag AG
English version © Floris Books 2013

British Library CIP Data available
ISBN 978-086315-948-0
Printed in China through Asia Pacific Offset Ltd

Cinderella

A GRIMM'S FAIRY TALE

Jacob and Wilhelm Grimm

Illustrated by Ulrike Haseloff

Floris Books

A mother was very ill. She knew she would soon die, leaving behind her second husband, who was rich but not kind, and her beautiful daughter.

She called her daughter to her bedside and said, "My dear girl, be good and God will protect you. I will look down on you from heaven and be near you."

After she died, the girl went to her mother's grave every day, and cried.

Winter came, and in the spring her mother's rich husband married a new wife.

The new wife had two daughters, who had pretty faces but mean, jealous hearts.

These new step-sisters took the girl's lovely clothes away from her and gave her an old dress and wooden shoes to wear. "Just look at her now!" they laughed. They made her work from morning till night. She got up before the sun, carried water, lit fires, cooked and washed.

The girl didn't have a bed; she had to sleep by the fire in the cinders. This meant she always looked dusty and dirty, and so they called her "Cinderella".

Once, when their stepfather was going away to a fair, the two stepsisters asked him to buy them pearls and jewels. Cinderella said, "Please bring me the first branch that knocks against your hat on your way home." So he brought gemstones for the two stepsisters and a hazel branch for Cinderella.

Cinderella thanked him. She planted the hazel branch beside her mother's grave and watered it with her tears. It grew, and became a beautiful tree. Cinderella would sit beneath it to cry and pray, and the birds would come to sit in the tree and listen.

One day the King of the land announced a great dance to honour his son, the Prince. When the two stepsisters heard the news, they were very excited. "Come, Cinderella," they demanded, "comb our hair for us, tie our sashes and fasten our buckles, for we are going to the King's palace!"

Cinderella did everything her stepsisters asked, and then she said, "May I go to the dance too?"

"You, Cinderella!" replied her stepmother. "Go to the dance, covered in dust and dirt? You have no clothes or shoes!"

But Cinderella still wished to go. Her stepmother tipped a great pot of lentils into the ashes, and said, "If you pick them all out before we leave, in two hours' time, you can come with us."

Cinderella opened the window and called,

Pigeons, turtle doves,
All the birds of the sky,
Peck lentils for the pot,
And leave the ashes aside.

Two pigeons flew in, then the turtle doves, then all the birds from near and far came whirring and crowding into the kitchen to peck among the ashes. They gathered the good lentils back into the pot in less than an hour.

Cinderella showed the pot to her stepmother, full of delight because she thought she could go to the dance, but the cruel stepmother said, "It makes no difference. You cannot come, for you have no clothes and cannot dance. We would be ashamed of you!" She turned her back, and hurried away with her two mean, jealous daughters.

Cinderella went to her mother's grave beneath the hazel tree, and called out,

Shiver and quiver, little tree,
Drop silver and gold down over me.

A white bird in the tree brought down a beautiful gold and silver ballgown, and silk slippers. Cinderella quickly put them on, and went to the dance.

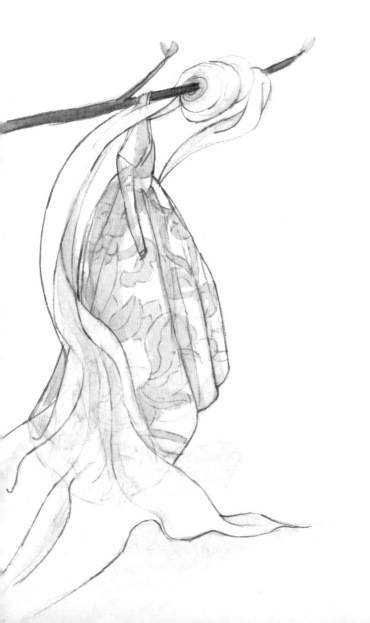

everyone at the King's palace stopped to look at the beautiful stranger. Cinderella's stepsisters and stepmother didn't recognise her because she looked so much like a princess in her gold and silver dress.

The Prince was captivated. He only danced with Cinderella, and never let go of her hand.

When it was late, Cinderella wanted to go home. The Prince was anxious to go with her, but she ran off so quickly he couldn't follow. In her haste, she left one of her silk slippers behind. The Prince picked it up. It was exquisite.

That night the Prince dreamt of the beautiful girl he had danced with, and the next morning he declared, "I will marry the girl whose foot fits this slipper!"

The Prince went from house to house throughout the land. He came to Cinderella's house and the eldest stepsister tried on the slipper. Her foot was far too big; she couldn't fit her toes into the shoe.

The Prince passed the slipper to the second stepsister, who took it away to her room. There she got her toes safely into it, but her heel was too large. Her mother gave her a knife and said: "Cut a bit off your heel. When you are Queen, you won't be travelling on foot." The second stepsister cut off a bit of her heel, forced her foot into the shoe, swallowed the pain, and went out to the Prince. He helped her onto his horse and took her away to be his bride.

But they had to pass the tree beside Cinderella's mother's grave. There sat a pigeon, who cooed,

> *Turn and look, turn and look,*
> *Blood drips from the shoe.*
> *The slipper was too small for her,*
> *Your true bride waits for you.*

The Prince turned and saw the blood trickling from the stepsister's foot. Shocked, he turned his horse around.

"Who else lives here?" he demanded.

"There is only the kitchen maid, Cinderella," said the stepmother. "You cannot want to see her." But the Prince insisted that even the kitchen maid should try the slipper.

Cinderella washed her hands and face and went to the Prince. She took her foot out of its heavy wooden shoe and slid it into the little slipper, which fitted perfectly. When she stood up, the Prince looked into her eyes and recognised the beautiful girl from the dance. He shouted, "This is my true bride!"

The stepmother and the two stepsisters turned pale with astonishment and rage.

The Prince helped Cinderella onto his horse and they rode away.

As they passed by the hazel tree, two pigeons cooed,

She fits the shoe,
Your bride is true,
Goodbye to you,
Goodbye to you.

Cinderella and her Prince were married that day, and they lived in his magnificent palace, where they were happy ever after.